The Night Santa Fell Asleep

Written by Katie Larson

Illustrated by Eva Rodríguez

Dedicated to my family and my mentor.

Katie Larson

"Time for bed,"
say Mom and Dad.
We rush right up the stairs.
It's nine o'clock
on Christmas Eve—
let's grab our teddy bears.

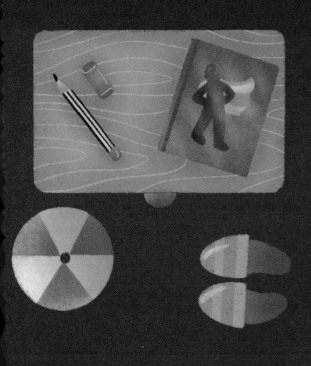

"I can't sleep," says little Kate.
"I have butterflies
in my tummy.
I sure hope Santa
likes our treats.
They're so warm and yummy!"

The clock strikes twelve, the house is still,
the tree's lit nice and bright.
A jolly laugh and jingling bells
sure give the dog a fright.

Santa steps into the chimney,
sliding down feet first,
ready for warm cookies
and some milk to quench his thirst.

He places all the presents
underneath the sparkly tree,
moving very swiftly
so the children will not see!

Santa Claus is sleepy
from his trip around the globe.
A few more stops,
then he'll head home
to slippers and his robe.

Santa sinks into the chair
to take a little break,
grabbing milk and cookies
and a slice of carrot cake.

He shuts his eyes to take a nap,
but soon the lights come on.
"Santa! You're asleep!
Oh, don't you know it's almost dawn?"

"Sam and Kate, I need your help!
I have presents in the sleigh.
I made my way around the world—
except the USA!"

"Let's go, jump in! Please help me out.
We'll do our very best!
We'll navigate the USA
from east coast to the west!"

The reindeer have been waiting,
and all nine are set to fly.
Kate and I jump in the front.
The sleigh will graze the sky.

From New England down to Florida
and all the states between,
we deliver Christmas presents,
wrapped in shiny red and green.

A fast turn to the left and through
the fields of the Midwest—
Santa and his reindeer do
what each year they do best.

Over the Rockies, through the clouds,
heading to the coast,
flying high in wintry skies
is what Kate and I love most.

"No time for breaks," laughs Santa Claus.
The sleigh sails up and down,
bringing gifts to boys and girls
in every state and town.

Six more states, a few more stops,
then Santa will be done.

He never could have finished
without three instead of one.

Hawaii is the final place
where we deliver the toys—
presents now around the world
for all the girls and boys!

It's time to get back home before
Mom and Dad wake up.
We're speeding through the morning sky
with hot cocoa in a cup.

The laughter and the jingles startle
Mom right out of bed.
Dad sits up and stares at me...
"What's that on your head?"

CPSIA information can be obtained
at www.ICGtesting.com
Printed in the USA
LVIC060351231120
672445LV00007B/45

9780578796451